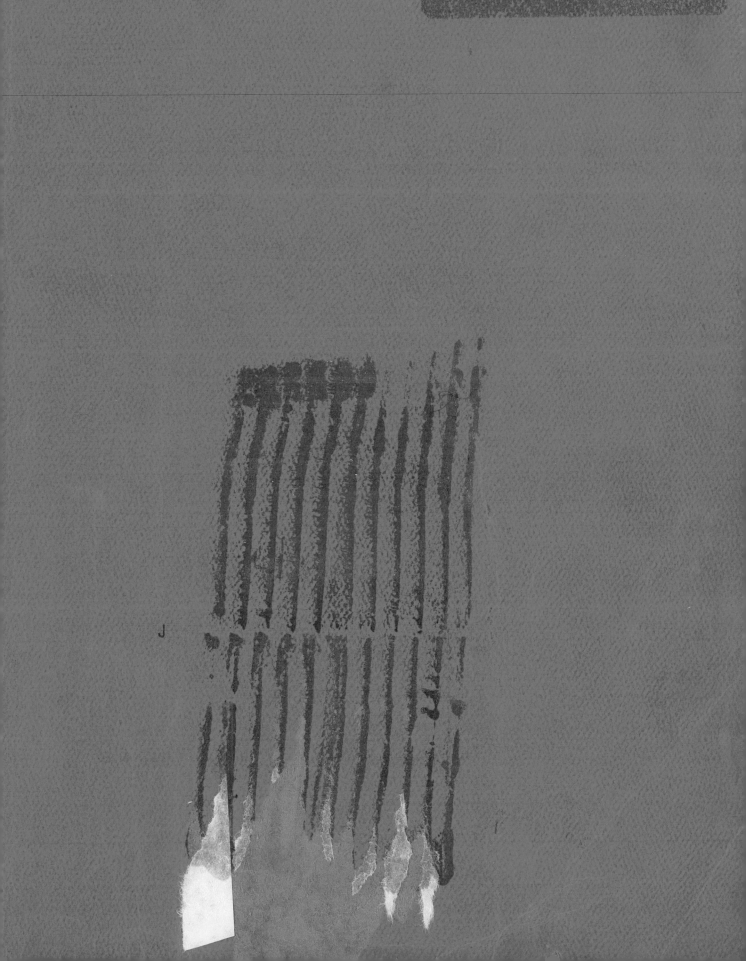

Harriet Goes to the Circus

By Betsy and Giulio Maestro

CROWN PUBLISHERS, INC., NEW YORK

For my Mother

B.C.M.

The text of this book is set in 30 point Baskerville with small caps.
The illustrations are pen and ink line drawings printed in black,
and background colors achieved with solid areas and tints of red,
blue, yellow, and black.

Library of Congress Cataloging in Publication Data

Maestro, Betsy.
    Harriet goes to the circus.

    SUMMARY: Harriet the elephant is determined to be the
first in line for the circus.
    [1. Counting books. 2. Elephants—Fiction.
3. Circus stories] I. Maestro, Giulio
II. Title.
PZ7.M267Har   [E]   76-40204
ISBN 0-517-52844-4

Harriet
Goes to the
Circus

The alarm rang. Harriet jumped out of bed. She hurried to get dressed.

Harriet was going to the circus, and she wanted to be the FIRST one there so that she would have the best seat.

When Harriet arrived, she was pleased
to see that she was the only one there.
She went right up to the door and waited.
She was the FIRST one in line.

Soon the others started to arrive.
Her friend Mouse was SECOND.
Duck was THIRD.

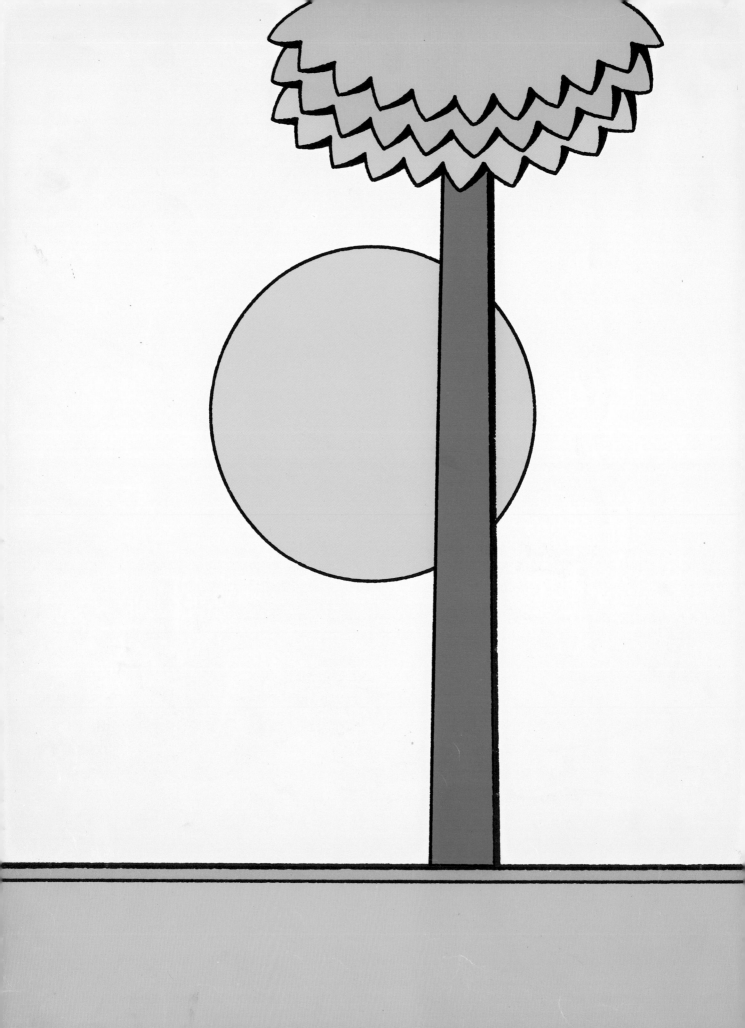

Monkey was FOURTH and Snake was FIFTH.

FIRST, SECOND, THIRD, FOURTH, FIFTH.
The line was growing longer.

Just then more friends came along.

Cat was SIXTH, and Lizard was SEVENTH.

Dog was EIGHTH, and Turtle was NINTH.

Then Owl arrived and was the last in line.
Owl was TENTH.

FIRST, SECOND, THIRD, FOURTH, FIFTH,

SIXTH, SEVENTH, EIGHTH, NINTH, TENTH.

What a long line it was!

All of a sudden, someone opened a door right next to Owl to let the animals in. Everyone turned around.

Now Owl was FIRST, Turtle was SECOND,
Dog was THIRD, Lizard was FOURTH,
Cat was FIFTH, Snake was SIXTH,
Monkey was SEVENTH, Duck was EIGHTH,
Mouse was NINTH, and Harriet was TENTH.

The animals all went through the door,
and poor Harriet was the last one in.

She was so disappointed that she
almost cried.

But just then Harriet saw the
big circle of chairs. No one was first.
No one was last.

Everyone had a front seat and, best of
all, the circus was about to begin!